I AM Media, International Presents

M others on *D* ormal Street

A Book of Short Stories by April Weaver

www.iammediabooks.com

Acknowledgments

To my mother, to mothers, to sisters, to brothers, to the children...
we are each other's keepers.

Love…

A. A.

Contents

"…to honor, to cherish…in sickness and in health; for richer or for poorer; for better or for worse…until death do us part…"

Ummph, folks are taking those vows for granted like they take the air they breathe for granted yet, cannot see the air or their own stupidity…far, far, far too much for granted as if love or air will always be available, ummph! What? They say statistics supports that 50% of all marriages end in divorce. Well, one should wonder, if those numbers include second marriages also, ummph! And, for that matter, why are there second marriages? Did death do the first marriage apart? Probably so, in many instances death of some kind took place, like death of trust, death of respect, death of love, then abandonment… Or, were those fruits ever really alive? Ummph, probably not or weak as hell! Just a shadow of moralistic fruit may be attending some folk's heart of mind. You know what I mean?

Like the idea is there, the seed is planted, but it don't grow none. Some folks just want to live by morals because they know it's the right thing to do, but sweet, healthy water in they cistern. It's like they soil done cracked hard and dry. And, some other folks can't live without those good fruits. Well, them two different kinds of people should never ever, ever marry each other… *"unequally yoked!"*

What? They say men give evidence of getting bored too easily. They begin to show signs as boys, no babies, to have high expectation, needs from their mothers, to be bossy and protective, and to have low attention capacity. They say that they are visual not forward thinkers when it comes to domesticated necessities. Their females must be willing to play the him game. They appear to be very watchful, busy eye balls especially of women. The male half of the species are image conscience and highly sensitive to their own fleshly needs, almost naturally hedonistic. What men is they talkin 'bout and who doin the talkin? People is either flowing a well of goodness they draw from or evil bitter. Nah, I do believes sometimes they sur- roundings help'em 'cide what kind of water they wants they well hold. Still we all decides fo' ourself one or the other.... Ummph!

"My name is Bessie Lee, I'm telling this story after watch- ing all the men I ever encountered, including: the 3 birthed to me, the 3 who married me and the few I dated, the 5 brothers I grew up with, all my sisters and friends' men, my uncles, and a host of those who passed by through this race called life. But, I see the women too they ain't foolin me. I see'em walkin'round showing all their grocery uumph! I guess the men's eye balls are busy you give'em so much to see, so they looking. I has some education because I not only watches folks, I reads plenty of books. That's how I taught myself better vocabulary words to say sometimes. Uumph, it's more than one way to learn so I learn some and got some learning to get. You know what I mean? But the women folk need to be a little more slow to speak, always ready to jump down somebody's throat with their words. Need to open up them ears and their mind and proba- bly need to close them legs a little more. Just so you know, my good words come and go. I say all the time. I got some more learning to get while I get more. I'm old enough to be a grand momma and maybe with the right husband...birth to one or two more, uumph! But, just listen here a little bit..."

So, let me tell you about a sap sucker named DaTin Flusher. Just in case you wondering why I call him a sap sucker, well, honey chile that's me being nice, you see. Just so you know, I'm gonna try not to cuss simply because it offends some folks, not because I don't feel it's necessary at times, but I feel it gets my point across extremely well. Some folks seem to think that other folks who cuss do so because their vocabulary is limited. Well, chile that is not always the case. We are not cookie cut. But, we do all have to answer to the Holy One! Holy and One both being key terms there. Well, my words might be a little bit limited but when I gets excited or angry I don't wanna always be searching fa words, so I says what I feel, Ummph. Every once in a while I slips out of my understanding, then I slips right back in though.

So, look at this fella Da'Tin Flusher. I don't know anything about how his family comes to have that particular last name, other than it was an old slave name passed down through some generations, not too long ago. This here 'round 'bout the late sixties, when this little black tar baby was born to a momma and daddy and siblings of 11 at least, from that one momma anyways. Along the way they finds out they got way more siblings than they grew up with uumph. Besides, they say that poppas are rolling stones. Well chile, I says they just plain ole rolling oblongs! See, that's me being nice.

Some of them can't allow themselves to love anybody for the real on the count of their oblong brain doing most of the thinking. If it's not the oblong it's they friends. Cause men folk show do love their cars, their friends, and what they friends think of 'em! Some of 'em anyways. So anyway, by the time Da'Tin come 'long to his momma and daddy, his momma had been hurt so bad by her husband, her children's daddy, that she wasn't mushy about his babies no more. He was though, she wasn't. He was proud when any of his women gave birth to his seed, especially Lilly. That was Da'Tin's momma name, Lilly. In fact, Lilly was over that super deep love most women falls into, although she still loved him. Uumph, it was that liquor bottle and dem so called girlfriends kept her going the same direction.

Nah, see, Lilly wasn't a small woman she wasn't large ne'tha. She was a short woman with plenty meat round 'bout her, mostly where the men likes it. Now, I'm guessin she stood bout 5'3 or so. Plenty tits, plenty back sides, some round da front too. What made Lilly stand out from the rest was that flawless dark skin, dem big light brown eyes, and her limba ways, uumph. That's was the problem too dough, dem limba ways! So, yeah, she kept herself lookin together matchin her colors, neat and clean and all. Hair always fixed nice wig or not uumph.

Nah, so she say that she named that baby as close to Satan as she could think of without being obvious. Let me tell ya chile what she says 'bout the night he was conceived. Says that she *'members that particular night very well.* Uumph, 'cause they hadn't had no sex in a couple of months and didn't have none again until the next one which was the 13th one, the last one, a girl was conceived seven months later. We look'n towards how it was DaTin gettin here though!

But, Imma go back jus a little bit so to show you how they both met and got togetha. Uumph, 'cause I knows folks ain't takin enough time to know one another and they show not taken 'em time to ask God do He 'proves and wants 'em to marry one another or no, stay the hell aways! Ask Him. God real smart 'cause He made everything we can see and them thangs we can't see too, uumph!

You see, Lilly hadn't graduated from high school, but it wasn't because she wasn't smart. Oh she was plenty smart, a quick thinka, memory like a elephant. I'm guessin his oblong and her oval did too much thinking for both of 'em, and before they know'd it somebody was baking in her oval oven. Nah, see, 'Nah, see, 'cause the very first time he looked at Lilly, he decided in his mind she was his and got her directly too, uumph! First date taken her to see a movie drive-in then he took elsewhere to a darker place and drove in, if you knows what I mean!

Dickson was Lilly's husband name, I would have to guess there is story underneath his name too but, I would have to guess at it because no one ever showed it to me. Nah, so Lilly never had to worry 'bout if Dickson was gonna bring money home for the bills, food, whatever they needed and many of her desires. All she had to do was say it and he would provide it. But, he just wouldn't bring neither his a-swipe, uumph if ya knows what I mean, his mind, nor his oblong home! Who ever knew where that Mr. Oblong was or with whom he was oblong-ing!! See, I'm trying to not cuss, but it's gonna come out here and there some jus a little bit. See, 'cause men that hurts their woman emotionally or physically makes me mad and they don't gets none of my 'spect, see. 'Nother thang too them kinda men lotta time makes them women abusers too with the children an other peoples to....make'em mean, cause they hurt so deep, see?

So, the night Da'Tin was placed in the oval oven, his momma had done stopped crying, cussing, and fussing about where in the hell he might be, it had been 3 long weeks! Do you know that's almost a month! Uumph! It seemed mo like 3 long years, she did miss him though. Besides, she had hatefully become accustomed to the lifestyle her husband had led them to and headed up they family.

Lilly part though, she was real good at what she did 'round that house. There was not no speck of dust nowhere you was gonna try ta find. 'Specially since she had a tribe of children that she run 'em like a army. Oh they was trained too, dem girls gets up in the mornin and they fixes they beds right up soon as they get out 'em, uumph even before go to pee! Then they goes and washes they tail, clean up right dem babies everything but they name! So, yeah, DaTin makin was somethin like a nightmare on Normal Street, see cause thats where dem Flushers lived. Uumph, it's anythang but normal though.

Lilly had completed her now famous Friday night fish fry. It had been the most successful yet. She had to send out for more fish 3 times before she finally had to declare no more cooking until the last Friday of the next coming month. Lilly made a little bit over a thousand dollas selling close ta ninty-five fish dinners at ten bucks. The rest come from soda and liqour shots, bout a hundred whisky shots at a dolla. I'm guessin the profit at seventy-five percent! Chile, see, I told you she what'n no dummy! Nah, she plenty smart jus mean. She needed some kindness, some love down in her well ta water her bones.

So, now you could hear da blues playing 'least a couple of blocks away... Humm huh, those mighty fingers plucking fury cross them guitar strings, ole Mighty Sam McClain sangin and playin flowing through the air along with the smell of fresh fried fish, *"When the Hurt Is over...baby you hurt me, and you know you hurt me..."*

Lilly stopped in her tracks for a minute, squatted did a nasty, dirty grind and screamed her, *"Amen!"*

Uumph, that the problem though, she amen to da wrong thang!

"...lost in da rain….oh, Lord...when da hurt is over, Lord maybe love will grow again…"

Swayed the music down Normal street past everyone ears!! This show made somma the neighbors mad, angry enough tah sin, but they never did, just mad 'em mad, mad, mad!

See, her fish fry dinners were the last Friday of every month, unless it fell on some special world holiday or something like that. She ended the fish fry at about 12:45 am, this time because she was tired. There had been a larger than usual crowd, guess word was really getting 'round. But there have been times they went on and on til 6-7 am in the morning, then have fish and beer for breakfast before the last of' em go on home, uumph!

She had been fretting awful bad about Dickson's disappearing act again, then pushing it down back in her gut somewhere, that's prolly where the mean grow... being used to it but that didn't stop the awful pain from oozing out though. That when the mean come out, but Crown Royal helped though. That liquor had a way of makin pain and anger go away, all but the mean, uumph that didn't go away. That mean started growing more an more everyday, though. She yelled louder and louder, she cussed more and more and she challenged any neighbor who dared to cross her little small, not so big self, everyday! And, every week she had a sure challenger! Uumph, a neighbor named Ruth Ayn! She came most every Friday with her sword called, *"Holy Bible,"* in her hand!!

That night the fish smell, the loud music, cussing and screeming was just too much for those who rested, read their sword, and practiced a certain kind of peace, a kind of quiet, see. Ruth Ayn wasn't 'fraid not one but *"Our Father which art in heaven…!"* She knows fo sure who gives each of us a every day! Ruth Ayn was tall though with her caramel skin, long neck and head held high. Mostly, 'cause she had good posture being tall 'an all, sashayed down to the opposite end of they Normal Street, ta see if Mrs. Flusher wanted some truth served with her fish an Crown Royal on dem rocks! Uumph! She walked along the side of Lilly 'nem house to the back yard where everybody bought they dinners, drink, and had their not funny or normal business going on taking place. She saw Lilly sitting in a chair not too far away, since the yard was long but not wide. She was positioned where she could see all the coming and going.

Now, so she sat in that chair or rather her backside was riding that chair like a stallion holding on backwards the way she was grinding to the way Elmore James so very finely caressed those guitar strings while singing, *"The sky is crying, can't you see the tears roll down the street…well, I've been looking for my baby, I wonder where can she be…I got a bad, bad feelin, my baby don't love me no more…"* Elmore crooned and Lilly grinded like making black pepper light as it could be!

Nah, she didn't give not no care who was watching when that whiskey got all down in there, down deep warming her entire soul, drowning her misery. She was mo grindin to his fingers on that guitar than anything else, cause everytime he stop sangin and concentrated on his wispy pluckin, she act like somethin hit her. She'd jerk her hips just a bit, then sway into convulsive winding moves like something was underneath encouraging that spirited rhythm. Uumph! Her children was drinkin and watching all this behavior from a distance learning what they was learning. The oldest one was 'bout 17 years and the youngest was 'bout 7 years and they was all drinkin, cussin, and doin everythang they saw them grown folk displayin, uumph.

He had been gone longer than usual this time without one word 'bout his safety or whereabouts. Why that man thought this was settling right with that wild wife of his, I have not one clue, nah. Well, maybe one. His oblong did most of the thinkin. Typically, one of his brothers would stop by with a word or check-up on 'em, nothing this time, though. Dickson had to travel for his job but it was usually overnight or the week-end not nearly as often as Dickson would like to have Lilly believe, *"lying assap spit!"* Is what Lilly would be thinkin and more, uumph!

Anyway, Lilly was tired and wanted to be alone in her room to cry or rest which ever came first. Her children were old and well trained enough to clean up the mess and put everything back in its place. Lilly was well known as sergeant mom, everyone knew how she ran the keeping of her house. Though she often took her frustrations out on her children, she really didn't mean to but, she did it all the time anyway. She allowed absolutely no nonsense from her children even when what she perceived as nonsense wasn't nonsense at all. And, because she wasn't getting real love, oh she got some sex, wild even, especially in the beginning, but we should know that ain't love right? But, even his slippery tricks had been coming up short! Chile, every woman knows, if her man ain't gettin it at home, he gettin it somewhere and some of them gettin it at home and somewhere any way! Uumph, shame, shame, shame!

She didn't pass out love and affection to her children nei

ther... just the mechanical, methodical motion of taking care of their physical needs. The only emotion she showed them was anger and its pain, and anything that come under them two. Soon after them kids finished putting the front and back yard back in order and cleaning the inside and went on to bed themselves, tired, well fed, and drunk like their momma. Soon after, their drunk daddy came tipping in so quiet, only he and God knew he was there.

He could smell the fish and pine-sol in the air, he knew it had been the day of Lilly's fish fry. Although he and his oblong had just finished fishing he still wanted more fish but only Lilly's catch nothing fried or laid to the side! *Sap sucker,* uumph! Lilly had not bathed, she had removed all her clothes except her bra, something she usually had one of the kids help her unfasten. She had lain face down sprawled across the bed in her drunken state, tired, and fell into a well-earned sleep when he tipped in. He could smell her distinctive scent from across the room, *"uuumm,"* he thought.

He tipped closer to her and rubbed the back of her leg down to the heel of her foot, she moved just a bit. He separated her legs very slowly, just a bit; she instinctively moved just a bit more. He stumbled back just a bit to unzip his pants, he stumbled out of them. The street light shining into the bedroom window was helpful when he was this drunk because otherwise he can't see in the dark.

Don't know how he steadied them legs to bend down a kiss her backsides softly, and real, real slow. Lilly stirred jus a little bit more. He stood and swayed back, he rubbed and rubbed away, uumph, now he was ready. As he began to crawl nearer to her, Lilly moaned and stirred just a little bit more. Suddenly she woke up, flipped over underneath him and promptly commenced to cuss his dirty, black assests completely out! If you know what I mean?

"Negro, where in the unholy pit of hell have you been? You black gunky sap suckin strangah or should I call you Mr. Black Sap Sucker Strangah?"

"I'm tring ta be nice, cause I been missin this...you baby, right?"
"Get your sorry bad-fishy smellin butt offa me!!"

He never answered her question but said, *"aw baby come on I'm home now lets..."*

"Dick, where you been huh, you ain't been here, your home, in 3 weeks you crazy to come tipping in here, cause I got something fo you ta get, alright?"

"Woman, I been getting all the money you don't mind spendin... forget what you talkin bout give me my good-stuff, I needs my sweet grocery right here..."

Nah, so they screamed back forth as they usually did when he returned from one of his long road trips, disguised as work travel. That's how those babies were made. He would go a business trip, Lilly was always suspicious, 'cause he had done made her very insecure in they relationship, it didn't seem to matter to him that they was married 'cause they was married.

But, Lilly was thinking, *"not this time forget him and his messy*

messy fishy smellin assests."

Yet, he was thinking, *"let me jump off in my good, sweet groceries."* Needin ta make sure ain't nobody been in his oval
cookie jar since he been gone... needed to cap off his great night
before he pass out. He was thinkin, *"this is my sweet, sweet
goodies no body else's not even hers, this is mine!"*

So, they fought. He kept trying to flip her back over, because he
preferred Lilly submissive as possible unless he says otherwise.
It was never bout how she felt about it.

"Lilly, shut your face up and give me my sweet stuff," a bit more
forceful, *"right nah, this is mine woman,"* he paused as he became more powerful over her, *"stop right nah, I mean it, girl!"*

He almost slipped his toxic oblong where only he wanted it
ta go, but Lilly would not keep still. Then they heard somebody
moving in the hallway, that's when Dick made his solid move
and flipped Lilly real good, pinned her down, real hard. He
let her feel the powerful control of his sincerity over and over
and over again. So much so, they both sobered up. They both
moaned. Lilly cried as she felt physically and emotionally torn.

She wondered, *"why her body melted with him, what kind of
love is this?"*

He was satisfied no one had been in his goody drawer while
he was gone away with his other fishies. He was so proud of
Lilly keeping his good, good, he wouldn't let it go. Lilly cried

harder... it seem to cause him to drive harder and faster. He wouldn't let go. His sweat began to pour, he really thought his wife knew he loved her. Dickson loved his self too, or so he was convinced, more and more each time his sovereignty reigned, *"oooooooooooow,"* supreme.

He passed out. She rolled him to his side of their bed. Lilly, rose, stammered to the closet, wrapped herself in a clean sheet, layed down on her side of the bed and cried big, hot tears before she fell asleep. Neither parent knowing that Da'Tin had started his descent. Their 11th child was on his way to the oval office that he was developing angry, evil, troublesome making and waiting a turn at hell raising like his daddy but worse, much worse! Yes, he will *show all sap suckers how to hurt 'em* when he get here, those where among his first unconscious thoughts!

As Dickson slept, Lilly had awakened, she thought about different ways to kill him. She had known for years that he wasn't going on business trips every time he was gone away from home for days or weeks at a time. Hell, some of his vexins had the nerve to come to their house when they were missing him trying to start some mess with her. She whooped all their assests when they had those crazy kinds of nerves popping up in their heads!
Coming to her house! Talking mess about where was her husband and the little sap suckers on their hips or in tow were her husband's babies. Uumph, what these vexins did not know was Lilly, as petite as she was a hell raiser herself and would take all her frustration out on them and their children without

hesitation. She was already kind of hard and her husband's cold brand of love turned her cold and mean. She had stopped caring a long time ago with that sappy kinda love.

All while she carried their 11th child she tried to get rid of it. She drank some sugar and water laced with turpentine, hoping it would cause her to miscarry. When her strong little body wasn't phased by that she just drank as much liquor as she wanted. But none of it fazed her body or the baby, as far as anyone could tell anyway. The baby boy, Da'Tin Flusher was born 9 months later, weighing 9 pounds, 8 ounces, 11 inches long. Skin dark like both his parents. When he was born he didn't cry, he just looked around. They say babies can't see or at least not very far at birth, but Da'Tin could see. He peered at everybody in that room.

His thoughts were, "*I'm here and none of you matter! I matter, that's who matters.*"

They also say that babies are born with a clean slate, meaning they don't think nothing because they don't know nothing to think. Well, this baby, Da'Tin Flusher, was looking, seeing, thinking, and making plans at his birth to be a surly bad assap sap sucker. If not the baddest among 'em.

Uumph, uumph, they say a momma can be so sorry filled, hurt, and mean that it carries over into her unborn chile. That's why ole wives tellya ta eat good and be kind to folks and ya self so your baby can be born healthy. I'm guessin it's some truth to it. Da'Tin, was a dark pretty baby, but what kinda man is he gonna make with all he been through already? You know what I mean?

Now, Dickson thought of his self as being a good man,

father, and provider. He made it his important business to be
at the birth of all his children; although he missed a few of his
outside kids' birth because they were either born at the same or
too close together and lived too far apart for him to attend each
birth. He would therefore have to choose one. But, no one
could honestly say that he did not provide for his children...
every last one of them. He had 20 at his last count. He wasn't
quite done yet either. I guess no one ever helped him to see
he needed to spread his love in the form of attention hands on
interaction with them children, quality and as much quantity
time, not sperm banking!

Nah, so Dickson was there when his mean baby boy was
born, making his 6th and last son by his wife, Lilly. Two weeks
later they left the hospital, Lilly's blood pressure would not seem
to come down. Dickson loved his children, especially those by
his wife, in his own way. He looked at this mean faced baby
boy and instantly had special feelings for him. They had argued
something awful bad two days before, see Dickson wanted to
name the baby boy Frank after his uncle, but Lilly didn't care
what Dickson wanted. In fact, she wanted the opposite of whatever he wanted with selfish reasons.

So, after they argued for 2 days about it, as soon he left her
room, she went on down to the records office in the hospital
and filled out the papers for the baby's name by herself. She
named their baby son Da'Tin Flusher and that was that! She
say that was as close as she could come to not naming him Satan without being obvious about it. He was their only child that
they did not name together. They did eventually, have one last
baby girl, who Lilly named after herself with his blessing.

Ruth Ayn, their neighbor on Normal Street, went by to take

Lilly and the new baby boy a gift. Some cause she knew Lilly had been drinking plenty liqour when she was carrying that boy so she wanted ta see for herself if the baby looked ok or if he might have the drinking syndrome some mothers pass on to their babies. Ruth Ayn bought the boy a stuffed animal and baby books. She brought Lilly a Bible and some bubble bath.

Chile, Lilly say, *"why you bring me this? You think you know everythang, don't cha?"*

Ruth say, *"I brought it to ya cause I know ya need it and I hope you know it for yourself someday. And, no, I don't know everything, but the Heavenly Father, nah, He know everything and made everything too!"*

"Look the next time you bring me something, bring me something ta drink." Lilly sad flippantly.

"I'll bring you something ta eat, the word of God. That's what you need more than anything. We all do!" Ruth replied. As she began to walk towards the porch steps because Lilly had not offered her to come into her house, Ruth Ayn also knew Lilly was liable to swing on her, then she'd have ta show her being a *"Woman of God"* didn't mean being a punk of nobody, uumph!

"I don't know what you speck me ta do with this but thanks for thinkin of me." She surprised herself and Ruth Ayn with that.

"Well, well, miracles never, ever cease, hallelujah, for all size blessings!" she said with a smile on her face as she walked on

down Normal Street to her own house.

As a baby, Da'Tin never cried much if at all. He made sounds to remind someone of duties towards him but not a cryer. He was a watcher. He observed behavior and people with concentrated curiosity. He did not miss much if anything at all. Da'Tin's eldest sister was like a surrogate mother to him. She loved him as if he were her own child. He went everywhere, except school, with her. He rode her hip only nine months, then he walked. He walked as if he knew where he wanted to go. And, he did, he wanted to go somewhere, anywhere, just could not or would not stay put, never content. Lilly was very grateful for her eldest daughter's fascination over this stern baby boy who never seemed to laugh or smile. Uumph, always serious, looking, searching for something, something he destined his self to never accept, and was sure ta never find.

Da'Tin was completely potty trained by 15 months, mouth full of teeth and sitting at the table feeding his self. People found him to be fascinating and creepy at the same time. Although, he knew how, he did not converse with anyone other than his sister-momma until he was nearly 4-years old. Once he began to talk with other people, they were astonished and somewhat afraid of his reasoning ability. Well, honey chile, let me inform you that Mr. Da'Tin Flushing soon turned that reasoning power into manipulative power!

He did not respond to anyone calling him, 'cept his mother, his sister-momma, and his daddy. Anybody else call him was completely ignored. He watched his mother intently as she bellowed out orders to his siblings and anyone who could hear that loud voice emanate from that petite body. He observed the robotic response of his sisters and brothers who never com plained or questioned her authority, at least not to her face!

Their household ran like a well-organized military base. Well, with the exception of Fish-Fry-Fridays and the other revelry parties that the family hosted so well! The Flusher children learned at a young age to rise early, clean, clean, clean, cook, eat, and drink quietly and never show they feelings! Yes, they took eat, drink, and be merry to its fullest extent and then some.

Some of Flushers didn't think the drink was enough, they had to fly higher than a regular, normal high. Some of the Flushers flew so high as to seek to die. I guess they held back all sorts of feelins too long. Flyin high, sometimes they landed and suffered consequences. The Flusher chilen taught each other one another's bad habits as if they were good and it became a generational pride. The men loved to have multiple women folk. The sisters never liked no woman for their brothers and was hostile always looking for any reason ta fight or ta instigate a fight. They didn't care as long as there was a fight. Uumph!

Soon, they grew and grew, there were quite a few to the 2nd and 3rd generations of them that born a higher tolerance of liquor and bad habits. Whereby, they stood a better chance at a better quality of life with more and more of they poisonous habits. Perhaps, their children will fare better later, not so much sooner. But, later on is a way down the road not travelled yet.

Now, so anyway, to go on, you all need to know this chile grew and grew. He was very big although his appetite for food was regular and by the age of 13, he could put away a 40oz of malt liquor like it was a sugary red kool-aide drink! Humph, and that was before dinner and sometimes lunch! I wonder how his liver felt about that, humph!

The day after he turned to be 12 years old, he had walked on home getting there just before the street lights on Normal Street had come on. As he 'proached, he saw his mother sitting in her *"Lilly"* chair, only on their porch. He was pleased with his self for making it there on time from so far away. As he 'proached the porch, bounced up two of them steps, that mean boy's mean mother asked him, rather told him, *"Where you think you goin?"*, she slurred hard and long like she fell partially asleep while speaking.

"I am goin in the house," he said cautiously in partial wonderment.

"No you not!" She spewed out her mouth, mo like a talkin snake than a caring mother. *"You a grown sap sucker man now, go find you some business!"*

They stared at one another with what seemed like a mean dark stare for several minutes before he walked back down the few stairs he had climbed and walked into the dark street not sure where to go. As he walked along he decided he would just walk around the dark streets and explore what goes on at night. Da'Tin was more tired and hungry than afraid. He decided to walk to his people's hole in the wall juke joint. There he could get something to eat, drink, and a ride back to his mother's house.

That long walk from the hundreds to the low end forties took him three and half hours. He arrived around midnight. They were in full drunken bluesy revelry. Da'Tin ate some fried chicken, beans and rice. He drank four shots of whiskey and chased it with that Blue Ribbon beer, took over djing until his uncle and aunt took him home. After, he told them why he was there, they just shook their head and kept on doing what they was doing. And told him, *"Well, you know you always at home here."* They laughed and partied on into the morning's dawn.

That boy grew and grew. He only seem to get along with folks who was a little affraid of him, the men folks, though. He didn't even get along with his own brothers. Most of them brothers were just too old at first, the one closest to his age by about 6 years or so, those two fought like starving arch enemies after the same last piece of meat. Not quite sure why, just plain old vicious I guess, both of them—all of them, uumph!

One of their street fights was so venom like, it was savage. Shame, shame, shame is really what it was, dem two brothers making one another bloody. What they doing, putting on a show? Do you think they mother tried to stop 'em? Nah, nah she did not. She watched like everybody else that was watching. Nobody else didn't dare try ta stop 'em. But, she just didn't want to, uumph!

He fared well with his sisters though. Them boys got along with their sister but not each other, especially the two youngest. Didn't understand dem Flushers at all myself. But, dem seem to be the only women that Da'Tin seemed to 'spect. Lilly became more and more reliant on her whiskey! The more her husband lacked in love and loving ways like quality time, caresses, attention to her well-being in general, the more she drank with her friends or alone listening to her bluesy music.

"Try a Little Tenderness," Ottis Redding sang to her, *"...I knew when we met* (pause), *I'd worry about you..."* she grooved on to another song. *"I been down one time, I been down two times,*

and now I'm drowning, drowning in the sea of love..."

By the third record she would be too tipsy to wanna dj for herself. Da'Tin learned to dj for the 'grown' ups, starting with momma by the ripe age of 5. That's right honey chile, 5 years old, he had got really good at it in no time. Told you bout Lilly's cousin and her husband who owned the hole in the wall tavern. Do you know, before I tell ya, that boy momma had that boy in that tavern as early as 15 years old djing on the record player for their drunk drinking behinds most every night of the week? Huumph, he was real good at it too, he knowed what everybody there wanted to hear before they scream out they requests. Little did they realize how he had studied them.

As a rule, anything he decided he wanted to do, he was excellent in doing it. The problem was he was reptilian, disguised ta look like a man, cold blooded! He decided evil was more profitable than righteousness, period and point-blank! And, so his life went. Back when he was ten years old, Da'Tin had the opportunity to make a double grade; he had been a straight A student for his entire academic career. His behavior record was clean because all the jumping, asset beating, and robbing of fellow students was after school, off school grounds. He struck so much fear in kids that they didn't dare tell anyone. Mostly, they avoided him with well-planned strategy.

Of course, he ran in packs, like most untamed street dogs. And, honey chile let me tell y-o-u, they were ruthless! They called themselves, *"The Silverback Killas."* They specialized in taking clothing, especially name brand dress shoes, from boys who didn't have back-up to help them once they were jumped, stealing cars, and breaking into houses. They didn't pick on girls, other than to lie through their teeth and take advantage of them sexually by coercion and break their hearts. Their greatest past time was stealing cars until they graduated to drug distribution.

Da'Tin wasn't interested in love, his interests relied upon getting money and people fearing him. Now, if you wanna say he loved money, *"for the love of money is root of all evil..,"* then Da'Tin loved money, because he thought about it all the time. He would do nearly anything to get it, didn't really want to spend it, would take someone else's, but wouldn't dare share his own. He would even kill for it…yeah that's loving on some money and that boy, was plenty evil. You could look into his cold eyes and they were just searching, searching but never content or satisfied. Cold is as cold does, freeze. But, you see, he could disguise himself like a chameleon and lie like the serpent himself! Oh Lord, Da'Tin was some woman's nightmare on Normal Street, waiting to happen. Uumph, uumph, uumph.

Sundown to Sundown

Sitting on the beautiful shores of Caye Caulker, Belize…
meditating to Jah…in awe of this great ingenious creation!
Mankind should be so much more grateful. I love peaceful
waters, they feed and soothe the savage beast in me. I need hot,
hot baths, saunas, and steam rooms for the best water taming
results, to melt away the toxins and everything negative. This
is obviously just a flesh and blood thing; the Heavenly Father's
Kingdom will not have bodies of water.

My grown sons; although still young kings, treated me, their
lovely mother, to any place in the world I wanted to visit for
a couple of weeks. In what seems like lifetimes ago, I always
thought I'd like to see Jamaica first. But, nah, I fell in love with
this place before ever seeing it in person. Beginning with how
the name Belize speaks to me for some reason. A lot has to do
with someone having had the wisdom to keep to a minimum,
man-made contraptions that make dirt or noise pollution.

Contraptions like cars, golf carts, boats or an overindul-
gence of skyscraper buildings, those things pump pollution
into the skies and into the waters below the concrete towers
like shameful concrete jungles. Mobile amenities only run
here once per day for drop off and pick up service of people or
supplies. To go anywhere else on the island you must take your
time and walk. The idea of slowly walking, with no hurry and
no worries for a while is intoxicating. I also chose this remark-
able place because I do not want to go anywhere that requires
me to be on a schedule, drive or be driven. I want to swim,
walk, sit, lay, all while reflecting. This gives me ample time to
rest my wearied, busy mind on how God has blessed me and

everyone. The sun and rain falls on the sinner and the saint, right?

It is mankind who has made the playing field uneven. Yet, still our Mighty Yah is always there, available. If only we could remember that life belongs to the Creator, and death isn't viewed the same as we, who inhabit flesh, view it. Death is a form of sleep. Sleep implies an awakening. Who shall awaken the sleep, you? Me? I may sound like I have all the answers, but I know I do not. Everyone who experiences this deepest sleep has time to rest in peace. We tend to think God is like us, instead of understanding we should be striving to be like God. Jah showed us how. I may sound like I have all the answers, but I do not. I have a few though!

After a long walk on these beautiful bright sandy shores, singing praises and dancing, I sit here sipping Moringa Mint iced tea, with my journal in hand, reminiscent on the triumphs from yesterday's tears, prayer, and praise that all brought me to this day. My beautiful age of 50 something. It had been so difficult being a single mother who kept the Ten Commandments, which includes dietary laws, cleanliness laws, weekly and annual Sabbaths. Oh boy!! Do you want to talk about being isolated, discriminated against? Imagine living to keep the fruit of the spirit: love, joy, peace, goodness, charity, and more, among a nation whose lifestyle is anything goes. Not to mention, the lack of male protection, misunderstood, talked about and hated…….. for trying to live clean.

Oh, and did I mention how fine I was? So beautiful that now, at 50, I still have quite a bit left over ha ha! My skin is still medium honey brown, my natural hair near my shoulders, medium large eyes slightly slanted at this point. No tummy, long legs, approximately 5'7," weighing in at 155, with curves in the right places, just a little cellulite in places only he would see if there were a him, ha haaaaa. I still have no wrinkles. I enjoy working out. Therefore, my muscle tone is decent, working on tightening it up though. Cooking and healthy living is a joy to me. Yet, even that can be viewed as, *"doing too much,"* as they currently say.

Yah's Commandments are not taken as a prevalent *"must do"*, so yes, honey, I have been there and done that painfully and prayerfully well! My sons were persecuted too. Actually, worse, because they were somewhat defenseless children if I wasn't looking. Two parents working together can't be aware of everything at all times. A single momma certainly cannot. Their earthly father was among the disrespected Black men, who dieted on the unfair hope deflating grub of the man in charge of this land's canned food. So unfortunately, he wasn't much help. Sometimes that fact made me sad, other times it made me mad. Please believe, my eyes were and remain open.

I remember how Friday, Saturday, and Sunday were like unto a world of their own to me. Our Sabbath preparation began Friday, before sundown. Yes, I learned as a young adult to acculturate my lifestyle, as much as I was able, to do what God intended for His creation, as I understood. It was exciting, invigorating and powerful even, but also lonely. Friday, so grateful for the approaching Sabbath, so I could shut down on the world and its nonsense, its cares. That's how I first began to feel about it. Yet, my life and understanding continued to grow and develop.

The more you know, the more you are responsible for, the more your lifestyle changes and is challenged. That doesn't change or stop because of one's knowledge or obedience to God's laws. It may or may not increase. Preparing for the Sabbath means buying everything you need, cooking and getting any cleaning done before sundown. This frees you up to rest, reflect on God's goodness and meditate. Convocation for the sake of spiritual re-strengthening.

Back in those days, one of the hoopties I owned constantly ran hot. I'd spent too much money for so-called professional Automotive Technicians to tell me they didn't know what was wrong. Why do I have to pay folks who do not fix the job they were hired to fix? Unmarried women get taken advantage of in so many ways, this is one, and by so many people, they are gonna have to answer to the Heavenly Father for that crap!

Thank God I attended college not too far from my sons' school, so I was able to arrive there an hour early and allow the car at least 30 minutes to cool off. I didn't have classes on Fridays, so I'd just go to the library to study or work on assignments while they were in school. This gave me 5 hours of uninterrupted study. Well, almost uninterrupted.

My mom was sure to call with talk about her needs or complaints about one of my siblings. I wish her life had not been so hard, she really had a lot to offer a kind man. Not sure she was open for a true strong man of God who was kind. But, just a regular kind Joe, who liked for his wife to give him lots of doting attention. You know, like cut the seeds out of his watermelon, watch him eat meals she loved to prepare for him, things of that nature.

Then there was that first love, who liked to pop in and out of my life to his convenience, while I prayerfully hoped God would heal his life. Aside from that drama, the car would cool for 5 hours while I studied. *Whew, finally seated.* I never knew I would like studying information so very much! Especially, Psychology and English. Little did I know Science and History would become super fascinating interests of mine as well.

I parked the car in the same place, Lot B, so I would not have to remember or wonder where I parked. No matter which building I attended class or the library for study, I always parked in Lot B, quite a distance actually. I chalked it up to aerobics. Study time over, I packed up my book bag of all my things that had been spread out on the table in front of me. Pack on my back, I began my 3-mile trek to the boy's school, gathered them up, and stopped by the store for a few bags of chips as a treat for them.

The store was always so wild and unsafe for my sons un-chaperoned, which is why they were never left alone outside that school building. Then, together we would walk the 3 miles to where the car was parked. After, in the privacy of my mind, praying all the way back to our apartment that the car would not overheat on us. During the days of the car running hot, we would park the car, empty our book bags, throw them on our backs, and walk to the stores another 3-4 miles away from where we lived. When we arrived back home, we unpacked our bags and cleaned-up; although, it wasn't too messy, before chilling out, in for the night.

The boys always took their bath or shower before I moved into the bathroom. My Friday night baths were always my best Bible reading times! When I tell you that was enjoyable, it's nearly an understatement. Like waaaaaay better than a *"Harry Potter"* experience, absolutely, had to be. Yes, halleluyah, the sun is down! Goodnight world.

Sabbath Day

Generally, I awoke every morning and almost immediately began speaking to God, most especially so on Sabbath mornings. The very acknowledgement empowered me to get the day started. The boys were awake in their room. Thank God for the large rooms we have here. David was reading or writing, Petah was playing his desk, making it sound just like a drum.

In the kitchen, making turkey sandwiches on wheat and the works. Washing fruit, bagging chips into baggies, paper plates, napkins. Everything ready to be placed in the big bag,

"Want some help momma?" Petah came and asked.

"Sure, bag everything up for us."

I nor my children were really breakfast eaters. However, we ate a hefty lunch and snacked very well, usually on trail mix put together by this mother's loving, picky care. Once we were dressed, we grabbed our Bibles, notebooks, food, and drinks and headed off to church, which we more affectionately referred to as, *"Bible study class,"* or just, *"Class."* We sat and read our bibles for approximately 3 hours, excluding singing, prayer, and announcement time.

I always kept my children with me. The children's bible class was attended to well enough, that's my nice description of why they no longer attended the children's study. My children and I were very close. Not in an obsessive way, in a close knitted family, I watch and train my kids and they love me as well sort of way, haaa. Even though we pretty much ate by ourselves, it wasn't because we wanted to, it was because they weren't allowed to run wild and I wasn't a favorite sister being single, divorced and all. Yes, so it was lonely inside and outside the gates baby for sisters like me.

We would head home, giving ourselves about an hour before sundown, back in the early days. Later through the years, we began breaking out as soon as bible study was over. We got so fast at getting in and out the door that we had it down to a science. We would arrive as the choir was singing, this gave us great escape of probing eyes or the too invasive questioning slash accusations. We would be sure to use the washroom during announcements and walk swiftly to the exit in the very front of the building. Less people exited using that particular exit. We also parked on the street, which allowed for an even faster exit from the area. We would usually go straight home, or sometimes we would go see my mom before heading home. I would sleep the rest of the Sabbath day.

Sunday

Everybody was so mad and judging the crap outta me when I stopped going to church on Sunday! When I stopped keeping the traditions of man's annual days, my family and friends thought I had literally lost my mind. They would not listen to my perspective, they would not read or research for themselves. They would only say the same old thing basically over and over again in the vein of *tradition* and how those days and times are about *bringing family together*.

Well, according to my research, those days and times are

about the winter solstice and were grafted into Christianity's religious beliefs and tradition due to bringing those people and their money into their control...Easter, Asherah or Ishtar... dates back to ancient Babylonian customs and observance of fertility, sexuality, it even delves off into sacred orgies and child sacrificing! I had absolutely no further interest in being loyal to a tradition that offends the very God we all say we love. *Why aren't people interested in being brave or honest enough to seek out God's perspective? How can there be an argument if the discussion utilized all the same tools such as the Bible and various other history books?* All these painful thoughts would torment me the one morning I had the opportunity to sleep a little later. Sunday morning.

One of several problems with Sabbath convocation is the praise and worship isn't as powerful as it could be. However, the reading of the holy word was nail on. Back when the boys were even younger, before Petah had begun walking, I could hear the boys moving about on Sunday mornings. Petah had made his way to bowls, pots, and pans under the sink. He had set them up all around him like they were his percussionist instruments and played them very well. Listening to his rhythmic prowess at 2 years old was fascinating and amazing, because he hadn't had time enough to have been taught. So where does this sort of natural expertise arise from? I had to get up at that point for sure because I could never guess what Petah would do after his musical time, I also never knew how long that time would last for him.

Now Petah's elder brother by two years, he was my quiet child. He was introverted, a deep thinker, he was reading already and not quite 4 years old. This kid talked about wanting to be able to read before he could clearly verbalize the desire. He would say things like, "*Ma, I wanna read so nobody will to tell me anything, so I can read it for myself.*" Or, "*When I know how to read then I can teach myself and I will teach Petah too.*"

David was always so serious for a little boy. I would actually have to trick or coax him into having fun. I mostly did that by running around with them outside, creating adventures for us to explore, and sometimes funny children's movies worked. The first time I took him roller skating, all the other children were on the floor skating, as I looked out there I didn't see him. I frantically began walking around rather quickly, looking for him. I found him walking along the wall looking at something. When I asked him what he was doing, he said that he was *"following the pipe along the wall wondering where it would end and what was its intended purpose".* That surprised me and scared me a little. He was only 4.

When I asked him if he wanted to skate, he replied that he thought it was *"silly and not a good idea for wheels to be on shoes".* Again, I was surprised and a little scared. Why would he be thinking of that? So, I told my child that I'd give him a dollar to try it. He agreed, but said he would give it back if he liked it, but doubted it. Well, he surprised me yet again because he liked it. I encouraged him to keep the money for a drink later. However, he did tell me that he wondered *"who thought of putting wheels on shoes!"*

We pretty much were routined for each day of the week, such was the life of a virtuous single mother. On Sundays I generally fixed a fun breakfast, like silver dollar pancakes. Of course, they had something healthy in them like walnuts, raisins, bananas, blueberries, or whatever was in season, on sale, or in the refrigerator. I kept old containers to pour their home-made tea juice in for travel. Sometimes I made hash brown patties. Whatever I made, it had to be enough to hold every-body's appetite for half a day. You see, what did not happen was buying fast food for our consumption. Also, it was conve-nient to fix easy finger food type breakfast on Sundays, because generally we only had a few moments if we were going to eat at home most of time. It was on the go.

Sunday was the day for the laundromat, grocery store, car needs, or any other household items or personal items we need-ed for living. It may not sound like much to do but try having to take care of all of that with two toddlers. Two children under the age of 5, crazy traffic, encountering people everywhere you go because as much as I may have wanted no one was obligated to move out of my way, so I could hurry to complete my tasks for the day. I had to merge our lives and needs with the lives and needs of others taking care of their own business. It was even more difficult during the times we didn't have a car. Al-though having a car could still propose its own set of issues.

I remember thinking as a child, no dreaming, *"...how beau-tiful and kind my husband will be to me and our children. He will be chocolate and fine! He will make a lot of money as a professional whatever he wants to be. He will love God or be seeking answers at least. And me? Me, I will be beautiful all the time, before and after each birth of our children, I will keep a clean beautiful, spacious home, and run my own business, yasss!! I will love the Creator..."*

I would often remember those dreamy days during my 30's, I still looked and felt like I did in my 20's. I would jog up and down 3 flights of stairs multiple times! Transporting toddlers, groceries, and everything all by my beautiful self!! Well, at least I could chalk that up to aerobics!

More questions ran through my mind like, *"Why is it that I, a beautiful Black woman, don't have a man, a husband? But, everybody else has a husband, a Black husband including other men! Where is my dream husband?"* Up and down the wood staircase first, with the children, securing them safely in our apartment. Then, 3 more trips to get the groceries and laundry. This was the first half of day 1 of my 6-day week. I couldn't even allow myself to think, *"I'm tired…Shhhhhhh, don't think it and don't DARE say it."*

Only once in a while, did I allow myself to confess being tired to a best girlfriend or my little sister. *"What? Yes, so we don't get a husband or a man for more than a couple of years, and we are not allowed to be tired. Nooooo not angry or we will get the 'ABW' label."*

"David, Petah it's bath time!"

Sunday night. I generally allowed the boys to take a long fun bath on Sunday nights. Our schedules were so busy, leisure time was precious, plus they rested better. Besides, next it was momma's turn! Yes, bath time for me meant my children were beautifully asleep. I could turn the radio up in the living room, so I could hear it in the bathroom down the hall.

First, I ran all hot water until the tub was half full. Once half full, I added a cup of magnesium, Epsom salt and 2 tea bags. When the tub was three quarters full, I turned off the hot water, turned on the cold water, and added coconut scented bubble bath. I had to bring a gallon of distilled water to drink because a whole lot of sweating was about to go on! I was also gonna need a couple glasses of sweet red wine, some fruit and cheese, and my candles. I rubbed olive oil all over and eye measured about a table spoon amount in the tub.

Candles on the sink flickered soft relaxing light, as I eased myself down into the really hot water. My feet were the first to feel the tension leaving. The more I submerged into the water, slowly, the more I began to feel stress loosen its grip on my life. By the time I would have my body fully emerged, relaxation would begin sweeping aches, and even some worries away. I closed my eyes to meditate on peace and a better blessed future, starting with a plan for the next day.

Ummm, I could hear Jon Mons' deep bass voice announcing what he would play next, *"...want some of your brown sugar... sugahhhhh..."* Reached down the side of the tub to grab my journal and wrote some poetry. So, this was how I enjoyed my Sunday nights. Soaking lasted for nearly 3 hours really. Jon Mons had one more hour before he signed off.

The wine had me even more relaxed, I climbed out the tub to go dance in the living room where the music was a bit louder. Shadow dancing on the wall and the shades was fun. I hadn't put up curtains yet. I was dancing with myself. Sometimes I would get back into the tub, and sometimes I would just let a movie finish putting me asleep.

The first spring we lived in the only courtyard apartment building on Normal Street. Many of its tenants were outside discussing various problems they were having in their apartments. As I walked out of the building some guy spoke kindly to me.

"Hey lil sis, my name is James, I haven't seen you around here before. What's your name?"

"I just moved into 3c, I mean we…."

"3c?" he pointed up to my apartment?

"Yeah."

He yelled over to his friend, *"Hey Ricky, this 3C right here."*

"Why'd you do that?" I said angrily and defensively.

"Aw, lil sis, I didn't mean any harm. We just been enjoying the shows, Sunday nights or most Sunday nights."

"What shows?!" I was about ready to attack, hit him with something big and hard. He saw the look on my face and was immediately sorry he said anything. He realized I somehow didn't know they could see my shadow and that I felt embarrassed or like I may be in danger.

"Hey lil sis, I promise you, you ain't in no danger or nothing like that. We was just enjoying the shadow dancing. You didn't know we could see you?"

"Hell no!"

"I guess that's over, huh?"

"Absolutely over!" I said with a mean look, while wondering how could I not realize if I could see myself on my side of the window shade, that others could see me on the other side of the shade!

"Ahhhhhhhhhhhhhh!" I screamed inside my head.

Ha haaa! It's one of many hard or bad experiences that have become hilarious now. The Most High protected me and my sons through that and so much more! We lived there for just a few more months, not a full year. We moved to a much larger apartment, although it was in the hood hood, we were happy with the increased space. Living on Normal Street had been anything but normal, on so many levels. It was an isolated period of my life due to choosing to live my life outside traditional guidelines or boundaries socialized by men. The portion of mankind that operates completely from a physical perspective.

I opened my eyes to this most beautiful array of orange colors. Huge, right here before my eyes, I never knew how many hues any one color could magnify. On the outside, a softest ray of orange, yellow begins its descension and fades down quietly, gently until a soft darkness moves in with a sweeping of cool air. I smiled at Yah.

Kings

There is a lot, really just way too much evil and foolishness going in the world. The world all over. Our world right here… The urban neighborhoods of the world. When people have healthy emotional intelligence, without any doubt, they know how to care for other people. I mean that's an automatic part of having really good emotional control. It's likened to a narcissistic impairment, the lack of care that allows one or many people to group think, to believe and operate from a perspective that it is alright to shoot someone down in the street. This simply because the shooter thinks it's an alright thing to do, like target practice. Those who judge in the so called, *"courts of law,"* deem the behavior acceptable. Unbelievably ridiculous.

Unrest was in an uproar, turning into an unsanctioned redemption of the urban communities! Protest had turned dangerous into out of control police, short of them executing a mass massacre. Especially since they don't seem to be interested in peaceful, respectful resolve.

"Disrespect us to death!"

A sociopathic nation of people does not understand or possess the emotion, nor the concept of love. Plus, as usual, the violence was instigated by the so called *"protectors."* Folks are angry, hurt and tired. But this time, they are thinking things through! Protests have been strategically staged throughout the states in ways that social and mainstream media has 24 hour coverage. Some cities have protesting concerts to raise money for legal fees, money for families directly affected by the senseless executions.

"Where is God?" some say.

"Always there," many say.

"Don't underestimate the Creator," many more believe and say.

"He has to be aware," say some others.

This was the social temperature in the era this kingly love was made. This situation isn't very much unlike the times before. There are always a few details that have been different, of course. Like, a young boy running to a store for snacks, or an innocent young man driving his family home from the grocery store after a long day at work. Another young Black boy running and playing in the park.

This time, a young teenager named Moses King walked home from the bus stop. He had been on his usual schedule of school, basketball practice, and one 20-minute bus ride home. Most times he didn't stop in the store right there at the bus stop. His mom was so adamant on his getting off the streets as soon as possible, that she purchased juice, water, and snacks by the case leaving him no need for neighborhood store trips.

Moses was fondly referred to as MK by those who knew him. His momma loved calling her son by his name, Moses. Although he was an excellent ball player with lots of promise, Moses was practical. He had a fascination with numbers, so he could just as clearly see a career in Finance and teaching young Black children math. He tutored a few students in the elementary he graduated from three years earlier. Moses' elder sister of two years was about to graduate in the upcoming year from the University of Illinois with a degree in Communication. His momma was finally seeming to relax some, she had been smiling more lately.

The Monday Moses tried to walk straight home from the bus stop as usual, something went crazy wrong. He didn't make it. A 30-year-old Caucasian cop with twelve years on the job was driving past in his cruiser. He flashed his lights, flipped his siren a couple of times, pulled abruptly in front of Moses and through his window told him, *"Stop right there."* Moses stopped but continued to bounce his ball.

"Where are you coming from?"

"School."

"Oh, really? Show me some id."

"It's in my bookbag." He flipped his bookbag around his shoulders to the ground, like most kids do, to go inside. But as he did his ball began to roll away, almost in the same motion he began moving to retrieve it. As this happened, the officer placed his hand on his gun and ordered Moses to stop.

Moses replied, *"I'm just getting my ball."* Just then Moses' big long foot accidently kicked the ball further away...in motion to speed up just a bit to grab his ball...he flew into the air from the three bullet blasts, before hitting the ground face down. Moses died instantly.

People had already been watching and although it happened fast, they immediately began running to MK's side, screaming: *"Oh my God!"*

The officer came out of what seemed like a daze and began calling on his shoulder radio for assistance, *"Shots fired."*

What the officer did not say was that *he was the only one who fired shots.* But he was right. He did need assistance. Because some folks was about to make him come up missing. The outrage this swelled into throughout urban neighborhoods nationwide rose to another level. In Chicago, this time, it reached the north downtown streets. And, yes, expressways were blocked in most major cities in the following weeks. In the midst of madness, anguish and the unbelievable depths of sadness, babies were being born, people were getting married, and love blossomed, still...

Blossoming love

He called her on the phone again. She was on her way home this time. She shared a luxury townhouse with her sister, who was only one year and six months older. The sisters joked about how since they were so close in age and resembled each other so much, with the exception of color tone, they can change it up and be twins sometimes. Take turns being the elder or younger, whichever was the most fun or convenient. Nonetheless, they were very, very close sisters.

They were each successful Certified Accountants, planning to start their own management company. They planned to manage and finance multiple successful businesses, including several of their own. These two young Brown sisters were raised by two highly spiritual, cultural, and socially conscience parents. Caliah, her friends called her Cali and Keshai, a.k.a. Keke, each shared their parents' idealistic views. Their unequivocal, decisive plans for their company were not founded on selfish gain. No, rather, it would serve as the for-profit business to support the multiple not-for-profit entities the underserved communities so desperately needed. They were impassioned when it came to their philanthropic pursuits.

Cali was medium tall, 5'7 weighing in at 158 pounds. Some say she weighed too much, however, she had so little fat and toned muscles, to the point of sculpted precision. Her light brown eyes and caramel skin tone actually looked like caramel candy, the kind on those candy sticks kids love until they are older and understand pulling taffy from their teeth is not a kool look.

Cali wasn't the type to keep her nails polished, although they were naturally pink at the bed and white on the tips and she kept them at a modest length. She also did not require, and therefore used little to no make-up enhancements. The young sister was beautiful inside and out. It had a lot to do with her genetic specifications. She was also very health conscious and very spiritual. She glowed.

Cali's sister, Keke, was the chocolate version of her, exactly. They were often referred to as the CC Sisters, standing for chocolate and caramel. Their dad made sure his beautiful baby girls were trained well enough in the Martial Arts, Hapkido Style. This reassured him and his wife of the girls' ability to protect themselves. It also enhanced their self-esteem. He also taught them unfair, no rules, no holds barred street, hood fighting, along with the skill of weaponry and how to turn common things into weapons. This he would have made sure sons knew, but he felt his girls were so beautiful to the male eye it made them vulnerable to predators. Black males were vulnerable targets for other reasons. Needless to say, these young ladies were natural to working out with or without the equipment of a gym.

Their equally, if not more beautiful mom, Aminah, taught

them to be women of distinct respect for their God, themselves, their husbands, families, and others. She taught them this by loving example and every teachable moment that occurred on a daily basis. Aminah was a soft-spoken woman who clearly knew how to express her perspective be it welcomed or unwelcomed. Especially, when it involved her children or other innocent children who appeared unprotected.

Once she was picking up an order of Whiting fish at a fast food joint, which she rarely ever ordered fast food. She would learn to cook just about any food she or her family enjoyed if she didn't know already. Aminah just did not take the preparation of her family's food as a light matter. Therefore, a stranger preparing food for the health of her own body and that of her family was a serious deed. This particular food place was near their house, and for some reason Aminah had a strong craving for some fried Whiting. She stopped on the way home.

These particular young males working the restaurant, of another particular nationality, were taking too long to complete her order because they were too busy flirt-lying to the two young Black girls at the side door. The iron bars were pulled across the doorway they were speaking through. Finally, when he returned to the bullet-proof glass with her order, she paid for it and after receiving it through the spinning bullet-proof server, she added, *"Don't you men have women where you come from? Where are you from, may I ask?"*

He stared at her blankly for a moment before understanding, he responded, *"Afghanistan."*

"You have women there, right, females?"

"Yes, sure" he said.

"Then you need to bring them with you when you come over here, so you can stop treating my daughters and sisters like prostitutes!" she said softly, but loud enough to be heard through the thick glass.

"Which ones are your daughters and sisters?" he asked baffled.

"All of them!" she retorted, this time loudly.

She was angry. She had heard stories of how they would impregnate young Black girls then either steal the baby by tricking the unsuspecting female or completely ignore and abandon the girl and child, sometimes multiple children. She walked off complete with the *'Angela Bassett'* move. She had seen Angela do the move in a movie after burning her husband's clothes in the Volvo in their driveway.

Yes, Aminah's girls were blessed with her beauty, their father's light brown eyes and a mixture of both their height. He was dark brown and tall, standing at 6'8", a muscular, educated, God conscious, Martial Artist. He was also an excellent marksman. So very protective of his family, more secretly active in the community uplifting than openly. As soon as his wife returned home that afternoon, he could tell something was bothering her. When she repeated what had just happened word for word, action for action, with a clear complete description, he crossed over to where she was standing and held her in his arms, before speaking.

In her ear his strong voice said, *"hon, for me I need you to never speak to another man in that manner. Please, for my sake, do not approach men with your emotional thoughts on what they should or should not do. If it's that important to you, tell me, allow me to handle it from there. Will you agree?"*

She didn't pause long before agreeing with her love. She relaxed in his arms and he made sure he felt her relax before he released his embrace.

"Feel better?" looking into her eyes.

Smiling now, *"of course."*

"Ok, thank you baby."

He left the living room and went directly to his office that he kept in their small 3-bedroom house on Normal Street. He phoned his friend Larry, who was also his attorney and told him to speed up the process to find his family their new home. They needed more space, the girls would be in high school soon, they would be needing their own rooms, plus he needed to get his family out of the 'hood'. He didn't have to live there to be an active part of the solutions.

Cali and KeKe's townhome represented their passions. The foyer was painted with a soft light mustard yellow...on the farther wall hung a consuming painting called the *"Rhythm of Life"*. Its yellow, brown and orange hues depicted black and brown men and women swaying to a music you could not hear, but could see throughout the beautiful seemingly swaying shapes. The living room housed some animal prints that welcomed and comforted those new to its space. The focal point was a picture of a Black couple standing inside of a book in the air, holding hands, about to step onto a cloud, blindfolded. It spoke of undeniable faith.

Their long dining room was more of a meditation/work

out space. The white floor lay underneath warm peanut butter colored walls. On one of the longest walls various words or quotes of inspiration were painted in eloquent sections in dark brown, with the exception of one quote in green: *"You must be the change you wish to see in the world"* Mahatma Gandhi. The ceiling was eggshell white.

Cali's bedroom was various textures with a color palette in hues of brown, touched with yellow, peach, and deep lavender. For some reason, Cali insisted on having one solid plain black wall. Keke loved purple. So, everything and color in her room was based on how it agreed with her beloved color purple. She even found a full-length mirror trimmed in dark purple. Neither of the sisters liked clutter, something in every space or spot to be covered. They liked for each room to be able to breath and be breezy.

The darkest thing in their living room was their black colored pit furniture that they pieced together over time rather than pay an enormous price to be purchased all together. There were four six-shelved bookcases on the wall several steps behind the pit. There, one would find two shelves of Bibles, a few Hebrew, a few Spanish, French, and the rest in English. Urban fiction, Business, Psychology, English literature in sorted variety, mostly Black authors.

"Helloo," Cali held the o sound knowing it was him, so happy it was him.

David needed to hear her voice, *"Hey babe, how are you and where are you?"* he spoke with care.

"I am almost home. I'm so happy that things are settling down

some but, I'm still hurt and angry that this keeps happening to us! It's so ridiculous, it's crazy, crazy, crazy babe. I mean my head is still spinning and it's been days. MK's mother hasn't even been able to bury her son. She has to be responsible for gauging when it's safest for the city before she lays her only son to rest! Unbelievable! This really has to stop you know?"

"Yeah Cali, you know I agree with you, but right now, I'm more concerned with your safety. How far away from home are you?"

"Just a few steps," she responded with a blush he would have loved to have seen.

Each day they had been apart made hearing her voice so much more special to him. Today, for some reason hearing her voice was even more different than ever. He didn't know why her voice had been so soothing to him, just now. After all, they had been separated even longer than this before when he had to make an overseas business trip that lasted an entire month. Yes, he had missed her tremendously and they celebrated by treating each other to specialty dates, one of which included a wine painting date. That had been fun, especially when they added a playful bet on whose work of art would get the most votes at a couples' party they would be hosting next month.

Anyway, Cali planned it for an excursion after they feasted on a delicious healthy meal she had prepared. The feast consisted of a briled slab of pink Salmon, lightly seasoned with fresh squeezed lemon, along with sautéed spinach seasoned with fresh vegetables, baked sweet potatoes, and homemade peach cobbler. A delicious ligtly sweet white wine to chase. It was perfect.

Cali didn't understand why it seemed as though today was

different, special. David's voice sounded more comforting than usual. She walked the last half block to her townhome. Cali walked up the four steps and let herself in. She could hear her sister in the kitchen, so she quickly walked to the kitchen to speak. All she really wanted to do was to lay across her bed and finish talking to her sweetheart. Keke was standing on the other side of their granite island, sipping Moringa Mint leaf tea, with pure honey and freshly squeezed lemon. One of her favorite tea blends.

"Hey sis, good to see you could make it home. Want some?" Cali gave her sister a side hug and kiss on the cheek. Yes, she noticed the smirk on her sister's face.

"Nah, not right now," she said pointing to phone, *"I just want to go lay down in my own bed for a change, that downtown lockdown was the worst!"* Walking the short way towards the stairs to her bedroom suite, she resumed talking to her love…

"What are you gonna do when you get in?"

"I'm tired but I'm probably gonna do some laundry, so that it doesn't get too out of hand," slowly walking up the stairs.

"I'm tired and need to do laundry too…I understand."

"I'll do some laundry for you babe, I mean since I'm doing it, I may as well."

"You would do that for me?"

"Sure, hon that's not a problem, I'm not saying I'm the laundry

queen or anything like I'm gonna do it all the time, but sure, I'll do it for you." As she landed the last step, she walked the few steps to enter her bedroom.

"Thanks babe, I have something for you. I had an amazing meal at a new restaurant near the job. It was the whole nine, so I had to pick you up a dinner. Got some for your sister too since yall like to act like twins." They laughed.

As Cali walked into her room she could see it looked like something was crumpled on the floor on the other side of the room. As she walked closer, she could see his coat thrown in the chair and soon saw that it was him laying on the floor next to the chair, not anything crumpled up at all. They both hung up the phones. As she stood over him and in one swoop dropped her purse, removed and tossed her coat over his, and folded herself down on top of him. They held each other, locked in a long warm embrace.

He broke the silence, *"Ummm babe, I have missed you. This feels good."*

She whispered, *"yes."*

"I had to make a decision, either go all the way home west of here or come here to check on you in person. I had to make a decision without speaking with you first. Is it okay that I came by without calling first? The receptionist at your company told me you had left for home...after having been captive in your office since all the crowds and dangers of the downtown area broke out. I knew it was time to see you...with my own eyes."

Still in their embrace. It wasn't tight, it wasn't loose, it was just unbreakable. They held each other, he had no idea how absolutely good this was gonna feel. It had been about a week since things began to escalate to the point where people were spending nights in their offices, rather than risk the outraged crowds in the streets. Although for the most part, the protesting was orderly, the police were the ones who no one trusted to be fair or orderly.

"So, babe, your dinner is in the kitchen." Still holding each other.

"Umm, thank you, I'm so hungry too."
David could not believe how deeply emotional he was feeling for this woman right now. He felt her all the way deep down in his soul. He knew he had sincere feelings for Cali, but there was something else going on at this moment. They held their embrace still. David was a rock. They had been dating for a little over three years, having had great discussions and good times. Still, this was different. He couldn't exactly describe it in words, but he knew in those moments they had moved into another level of their relationship. This was a moment, a once-in-a-lifetime-moment and he had to speak to God.

"God, Heavenly Father, this is the one. Father I love this woman, please, can I have this woman? I will take care of her, I will protect her, I love her. Father I feel her in my heart, in my soul. May I please have her?"

When Cali heard those words whispered past her ears to God, she was more than moved. The chills, the sensations she felt was like unto a disintegration and regeneration at the same time. Simply mind blowing. All this in one embrace, and they were ful ly dressed. A warm tear ran down Cali's temple onto David's neck and some slowly evaporated, while the rest melted into the small brown pillow under his head.

He slowly tilted her head toward him as he reached down to meet her lips with the warmth of his. He parted her lips, it was as if they were fusing together in slow motion. He was hot for her, he wanted to comfort her and this heightened his senses for her. As they kissed so deeply and so soft, they felt like one, fully clothed. It was like unto a spiritual fusing.

Cali exclaimed a soft moan as she disintegrated into his energy, any tension vanished completely away. Time stood still. No one, no other thing existed. It was more than beautiful. They both knew they were each other's. He her male, she his female. They were flying as they lay there in each other's arms feeding each other pure love energy. Her sister stood in the doorway for a while before deciding not to walk away, but to speak.

"Dang, I feel y'alls' heat all the way ova here! I guess we will be planning a wedding soon?"

They held their kissing embrace for another moment before un-latching, each smiling, each comforted, he said looking into Cali's eyes, *"I hope so."*

Cali replied, *"me too."*

Keke pumped her fist and yelled, *" Yes, I love weddings...and yes, I will be your maiden of honor!"* as she sashayed away.

They only adjusted their embrace a little as David said, *"so I guess you will be my laundry queen."* They both laughed softly.

"And what kind of king will you be to me?"

"Your everything king, my queen. Until the King of Kings re-turns," he said without hesitation.

"I love you so much baby. You enrich me, we complete one an-other's circle. I have no doubt you are my one and I am yours."